A Fairy Tale of the Future

The Three Little Bots

Created & Illustrated by Steve "Supersonic" Harpster
Written by Scott "Space Cadet" Nickel

Published By BENDON Publishing, Int'l.
Ashland, OH 44805

This is the story of three little bots: a green bot, a yellow bot, and a purple bot. The three little bots lived on a planet where the sun shone almost all the time, and it was dark just nine-and-a-half minutes a day.

The little yellow bot liked to sing.

The little purple bot liked to dance.

And the little green bot liked to do long division. The green bot was a little weird.

There was someone in the galaxy that didn't like the three little bots. And that someone was the Big Mean Metal Muncher. He lived on an asteroid in cold dark space and watched the three bots through a giant telescope.

"I eat little bots for breakfast!" he would say.

Why was the Big Mean Metal Muncher so mean? Some people think it was because his underwear was two sizes too small.

The little green bot had heard about the Big Mean Metal Muncher, and he told the other bots they should all build spaceships so they could escape if the Muncher attacked.

"That sounds like a big chore," said the little yellow bot.

"Yeah, even worse than cleaning our rooms or changing the cat's litter box," whined the little purple bot. But they agreed to do it.

The little yellow bot quickly
built a paper spaceship that was held
together with bubblegum.

"There!" said the yellow bot. "Now
I can get back to my singing. I'm going
to be a famous rock star someday."

The green bot just sighed and went
back to doing his long division.

Next, the purple bot hastily built a spaceship of cardboard and tape.
"Building this spaceship is interfering with my dancing," the purple bot said.
"I'm working on some hot new moves for the Boogie Bot dance contest."

The little green bot shrugged his shoulders and started working on his spaceship. It was big and shiny and made of steel. It had dual rocket engines, deflector shields, a kitchen, and an indoor pool.

Suddenly the Big Mean Metal Muncher zoomed down from his asteroid and landed right next to the little yellow bot.

"I eat little bots for breakfast!" the Muncher roared as he gobbled up the paper-and-bubblegum spaceship. CHOMP! CHOMP! CHOMP!

"Yum! Cherry-flavored," he said.
The yellow bot ran away as fast as
his little bot legs could go.

He ran to the purple bot's ship, with the Big Mean Metal Muncher close behind.

The Muncher gobbled up the cardboard-and-tape spaceship. CHOMP! CHOMP! CHOMP!!

"Mmm," he said. "I like a little roughage in my diet."

The yellow and purple bots ran to the big metal spaceship. The green bot opened the double-thick steel security door and let his two terrified friends inside.

The Big Mean Metal Muncher was right behind them.

"Chill out, guys," said the little green bot. "This ship is 100% Big Mean Metal Muncher-proof."

"I eat little bots for breakfast!" The monster yelled as he chomped down on the shiny ship. CRACK!

"Ow!" he cried. The steel was too hard for him to bite through. The Muncher roared. "Let me in, you foolish bot!"

"You're big and you're smelly, so we think not," chanted the bots.

This made the Muncher very mad, even madder than when his underwear shrinks in the dryer.

"I'll find a way to get inside that spaceship," he said and came up with a plan. He quickly put on a disguise.

"Pizza delivery for the little green bot!" the disguised Muncher said.

"I didn't order pizza," the little green bot replied.

"Let me in, you foolish bot!" the Muncher roared.

"You're big and you're smelly, so we think not," chanted the bots.

"Argh!" the Muncher growled.

The Big Mean Metal Muncher tried lots of disguises to fool the bots.
"Congratulations, Mr. Bot, you've just won ten million dollars!"

"Special toy delivery!"

"Look! Look! Free kittens!"

"You say you're big,
you say you're mean,
but you're the lamest
thing we've seen," said
the little bots.

"Argh!" the Muncher
growled again.

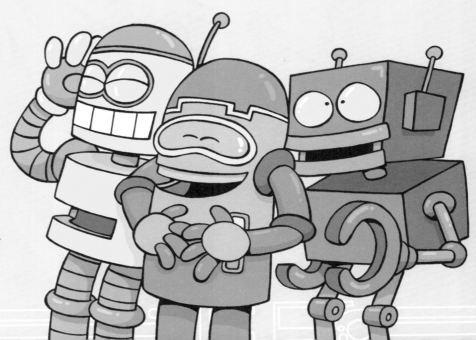

"That old monster can't get us in here," said the yellow bot. "But what happens when we go outside?"

"Not a problem," said the green bot. "I've equipped my amazingly cool spaceship with this state-of-the art Shrink-O-Matic Ray (not available in stores). Observe!"

The machine clicked on, and the Muncher was bathed in a strange green light and began to grow smaller and smaller and smaller.

The green bot laughed. "The Big Mean Metal Muncher is now the
MINI Mean Metal Muncher."